JEWELS EROTICA

VOL. II

JEWEL ALYSSA

Erotic/Romance

Cover image: Pixabay.com

Cover Design: HRK

This is a work of fiction. Names, places, incidents and characters are the product of the author's imagination or used in a fictitious manner. Any resemblance to actual persons, living or dead is entirely coincidental.

No part of this book may be reproduced, distributed or transmitted in any form or by any means including photocopying recording or any other methods without the permission of the author.

Author can be reached by mail.

Jewelalyssa93writer@gmail.com

<u>WARNING 18+</u>

This book contains mature content, explicit erotic scenes and language.

Table of contents

Desperations

I am a single man who just came back from Dubai. I was working there as a supervisor.

After my two period completed I came home for a two month leave.

I am a shy guy though I look smart.

My parents went for a week retreat and I had to go my room mates' houses to deliver the packages they gave me.

I started with nearby distances. Almost every package I delivered and there was only one left.

This one was a big package. It was for a friends' wife and his newborn child.

I went after having breakfast in a plan to be back at home before night. I had to travel so many kilometers and unfortunately there was an accident on my way.

It consumed a lot of my time.

It was a difficult task to fine their home as I lost the track at least three times.

I could only reach there at dusk.

I met my friend's mother and his wife, Mansi. To my surprise she was my old school friend. I had a little crush on her.

Well, all the boys had crush on her. She was a damsel.

My friend's mother was too old and sickly. I should say Mansi had a tough job to maintain the house, looking after her old mother in law and now her six month old child and all the household chores.

She left her job to be a full time homemaker after three months of marriage.

Her mother I law wasn't in a good condition and they requested me to stay there at night just in case if they had any emergency at night.

I had no choice. Besides I can secretly watch my old crush.

We talked a lot about our school days. It seemed she was so happy to see me. She was getting bored at home.

We had dinner together. I helped her in her kitchen works as we chatted continuously.

At night the issue was where will I sleep? There were only two rooms. One was used by the old lady. That room had a foul smell. The second was using by Mansi.

Finally we decided that I will sleep in Mansi's room. She will sleep on the bed with her child and I will sleep on the floor.

Her room had an amazing fragrance of lily. She always wore lily based perfumes at school.

What was I feeling? First time in my life I was feeling comfortable around Mansi.

At the same time there was a wave of nervousness in my heart.

She told me to sleep on the bed as I am the guest. And besides that would be better for her to look after the child.

I lay on the bed. She at the edge facing away to breast feed her child.

I looked at her back. Her long jet black cover was open and spread across her back.

I wished to kiss her.

After breast feeding, she laid her child on the mattress on the floor.

She looked at me and asked. "Hari, you slept?"

I closed my eyes before she finished feeding. I didn't reply.

I heard the bathroom door opening and closing after a few minutes and then the sound of water falling down.

She is bathing!

She is naked, uff. The thought sent chills down my spine.

The sound of water stopped after a while. I opened my one eye a little and looked at the bathroom door and waited.

The door was opened and she came out.

She was only in a bath towel wrapped around her. Top half of her breasts could be seen. The towel was too short. If I had slept on the floor I could have seen her cunt lips. I felt my veins heating up. All the heat went to one particular position, between my legs. My cock was hardening.

I wished for something and ohh fuck, it happened. She dropped the towel onto the floor. She stood naked with her back facing me. Ohh, what a butt she has. My cock was harder.

Turn around, I whispered in my mind. I wish to see her cunt. I am sure it will be as beautiful as she is. Will she be shaved or hairy?

It didn't matter though. Seeing a pussy in real life was a big deal for me.

I was feeling desperate.

She pulled up a knee length cotton pants with floral design. She wore a grey top which had a full length zipper in the front.

I was sleeping at the far end of the bed and surprisingly she slept at the other end looking down at the toddler.

Her lily fragrance hit my nose hard.

I moved closer to her as if turned in the sleep. My hand rested too close to her body. She twitched a little and her ass brushed my hand.

She turned and lay on her back with one of her ass on my palm.

Ohh, it was so soft.

I wished I could squeeze them.

She turned towards me freeing my palm.

"Hari are you really sleeping?" she asked.

I didn't reply.

Next instant she grabbed my cock and pressed tightly.

"Uff." I jumped up.

"What the…"

"Fuck me." she said in a sultry voice. She pulled the zip down. Both her breasts were visible to me now. She removed the top. My cock was throbbing inside my trousers.

Since pregnancy she didn't had sex. Her husband went to Dubai when she was two months pregnant.

I was confident now. "Will you suck my cock?" I asked.

"Show me."

She doesn't need to say again. I stripped all my clothes and lay naked on the bed. My rod was towering skywards.

She was desperate and hungry.

She mouthed my cock and started sucking like crazy.

Just within two minutes I came. My cream was all over her mouth.

Well, we both were disappointed.

"I never took my husband's cum in my mouth. Yours is the first."

"I am sorry. It wasn't intentional. I couldn't control." I apologized.

"You are a virgin, aren't you?"

I shook my head.

She went to the bathroom to wash her mouth and came as I went to clean my cock.

"I will teach you." she said.

We kissed.

My lips trailed over her face kissing her eye lashes, her forehead, her long nose, her chubby cheeks and her lips.

Our tongues intertwined in a sensual union.

I wanted this night to be remembered.

I softly squeezed her tits and drops of milk oozed out.

Suddenly the child started to cry. She took the child and started to feed. I looked at her child sucking her breast. I sucked the other and drank some milk.

Then I started kissing her legs. I sucked her toe and licked her feet.

My tongue gradually came up licking her thighs. She asked me to slow down as she was feeding the child.

I wanted to see her cunt. I was desperate for the most beautiful sight.

I made her stand and removed her pants. She had hair all grown but the sight made me hard again. It shook as she looked at my cock.

She shifted her kid to the other breast as I kneeled down to kiss her cunt. She kept her legs wide. I saw her beautiful cunt lips. I sucked and nibbled her pussy lips as she moaned.

I fingered her as a sensual excitement filled me. I rubbed her clit with my thumb.

I looked again at her cunt. Her hair was curly and her lips were deep pink. The whole sensual area was a little swollen.

I smelled and the lily aroma mixed with her wet cunt scent pervaded my nostrils.

Then I kissed her ass when she walked away. She went to lay her kid on the bed and secured with pillow on both sides.

She lay on the bed with her legs open.

I nibbled her breast and poured the milk on her pussy with my mouth. I licked the cunt with so much love and she moaned continuously.

I poured some milk again on her cunt and some on my cock and entered her.

I rammed inside her with all my might. What a pleasure? I was fucking a girl for the first time. I never knew fucking gave so much delight.

I was riding her cunt with ease. My hips moved with rhythm. I squeezed more milk out of her tits.

"Fuck me hard, Hari." Mansi moaned.

My thrusts became faster and soon I came inside her. I stroked as I let all of my cum fill inside her cunt. My hot cream was in her lake. I kissed her lips and said. "I love you. I always loved you since school."

"I liked you too." She replied.

"I wished you would propose me."

I was stunned to hear that.

We fucked again at 3 am when the child woke up again.

In the next two months I visited them many times, stayed at their house and fucked Mansi number of times.

Our relationship was growing.

*****_____*****

******_______******

Invitation

My name is Shivdas. But I am usually known as Unni. I am 26 years old.

I work in a footwear show room in accounts section. There were nine other people working here other than me, five people at the ground floor and four on the first floor.

Shreya is my accounts partner. She is 24 with normal height and with features matching her height. She is fair. She is married. She is hot. Her lips were blood red. Her breasts were little bigger than normal. She had a great ass. Her perfume was tantalizing.

It was given to her by her husband who works abroad. No kids and living with her in laws.

My cock always gets hard when I see her. But I tried to control my urges. I gently brush it above my trousers.

Why the fuck are you making me crazy? I usually ask in my mind.

We always sat next to each other at the cash counter and it was hard for me to control my rod. I used to jerk off in the bathroom thinking about her.

She became my desire. I badly wanted to fuck her. But I know that would never happen. I decided to approach when I get a chance.

One day she accidentally dropped her pen to the floor. It fell between my legs. I was busy typing the entries and she had no other option but to pick it herself.

She kept her hand on my upper thighs so close to my cock and pulled. She leaned down pressing her tits on the lower part of the thigh and picked up the pen.

My cock became too hard that I afraid it will push out of my trousers. Her tits felt heavenly.

I wished if she had kept it for more time. I looked at her face but it was unemotional.

Half an hour later I dropped my pen purposely between her legs.

I groped her thigh too high as my little finger was on the edge of her panties.

I bent down and my head touched her tits. I lifted the pen from the floor and raised my head rubbing her tits.

She said nothing and I was sure that she thought the act was unintentional.

The next day new stock came as the festive season was approaching.

Only both of us were in the go down to check the stock entries and attaching the price tags. No one will come until we finish our work.

This is the chance. I thought.

While attaching the price tags I brushed her thighs many times.

She may have thought that these were not deliberate touches and so she wasn't reacting.

I asked her to take an item for me. While she was picking up the shoe box I kept my hand on her thigh and squeezed gently.

"Unni, concentrate on your work." She said. To my surprise she wasn't angry. That gave me dare to try more.

I leaned closer to her face and blew some hot air from my mouth while my hand brushed her thigh.

"No." her voice was low. I saw her breast rising up and down faster.

I moved my hand closer to her sacred area while she was continuously listing the entries as I told her the batch number.

My hand was almost closer to her cunt, she made me stop.

"Unni, please don't."

I pulled my hands back but was now on her tits.

"Please, someone will see." She looked around.

"So you are worried about anyone seeing. If not, then it is okay for you." I shrugged.

She snickered in reply.

"No one will be coming. Even if anyone comes we will hear the footsteps before the person."

I was about to unbutton her shirt that we heard footsteps.

It was our boss' wife, Akhila.

"Hope you are not bored." She asked.

"No madam." Shreya replied.

"We are talking to each other and so we are good." I supported her.

"Everyone went to have lunch. I also came here to inform you that two more fresh stocks will be coming tomorrow."

"Okay madam." We shook our heads.

"I am going home now." she said and left.

Right after she left Shreya took my hand and kept it on her breasts. That was unexpected of her but I really liked her for taking the initiative.

I used both my hands and moved to her back to squash her melons. I unbuttoned her shirt and pressed her tits over her white bra.

My hard cock was touching her back. She gasped.

I made her stand and we went into a dark corner of the room.

I undone her jeans and inserted my fingers inside her panties.

I felt the heat of her cunt inside the panties. My rod was hard against her ass. I was kissing the nape of her neck as her hand dug inside her hair. She bent her head back and rested on my shoulder.

She took her hand behind her between our bodies and patted over my cock.

I pulled her panties down and my fingers trailed over her slit. One of my disobedient fingers entered the restricted area. I felt her moisture on my fingers. She was heated up.

She has already unzipped my jeans and took my rod out. She stroked it gently.

I was playing inside her cunt. My fingers went in and out in quick intervals. I heard her soft moans. Her sensual voices fired me up.

I removed her jeans and panties. She was completely naked down.

I stroked again inside her cunt while my other hand rubbed her clit.

She came in my hands. Still I didn't stop. "Oh yes, enough." She said.

She stood behind me now and stroked my cock. Her breasts were pressed against my back.

Her hand moved fast and my cock squirted out the cream.

We dressed up and started walking out when Indu showed up. "Aren't you guys going to have lunch?" she asked.

"We are coming." We said in a single voice.

Afternoon was uneventful but we enjoyed out time together.

She promised me to call in the evening.

She called me at 10.30 pm.

"Unni what are you doing?"

"I am at home thinking about you."

"Can you come here?"

"Now? Why?"

"Just come. I will tell you everything."

I knew this was an invitation. I wasn't going to refuse it.

"Give me a missed call when you reach."

I pushed my bike for almost 100 meters away from the house and started the engine.

I parked the bike in a plantation field little far from her house and walked under the shades.

I gave a missed call when I reached behind the house near the kitchen door.

I heard the door open and a soft voice of invitation. "Come in."

I went in. the whole world was under darkness.

A hand pulled me somewhere into the interiors of the house.

We stopped and I waited in the dark knowing nothing about what was happening.

The room was lit in an instant. I saw her standing naked in front of me.

"Ohh fuck."

It was the best ever sight to my eyes.

Shreya looked like a marble statue perfectly crafted.

My cock stood erect under my lungi making a tent in front of me.

"Where are the others?"

"They went to hospital as my uncle met with an accident."

"Why didn't you go?"

"Don't you remember what Akhila madam said? Two more stocks will arrive tomorrow."

"Are you going to sleep alone?"

"No. you are here to sleep with me."

She leaned onto me pressing her tits against my chest.

I wrapped my hands around her. My hard rod was knocking its head at her cunt lips looking for an entrance between her legs.

I lifted her head and sucked her red lips. I pushed my tongue into her mouth.

I felt her hand sliding down; she grabbed my cock and stroked it.

I groped her tits and started to crush them.

She kneeled before me after removing my lungi and throwing it to some corner of the room.

She mouthed my throbbing cock. She licked and sucked and nibbled my balls. I don't remember what all things she did with my cock. She was crazy.

"Uff… aah" I swirled in my position.

I made her stand up and kissed her tits. I sucked her nipples like a toddler.

I sucked down between her thighs slowly rising towards her cunt. I licked the slit and opened the cunt lips. Uff, the fragrance of her cunt entered my nostrils driving me wild.

I nibbled her clit as my hands clutched her from behind. Her ass got squeezed by my hands while her cunt lips were in my mouth.

My cock was jerking as it was signaling for action.

I took her to the bed. I climbed on top of her and rammed into her cunt.

"Aaaahhhh." She made a soft scream as she arched her back.

I pulled my cock out and then rammed into her again with more force.

"Aaaahhhhhh." She creamed louder.

I closed her mouth and started playing slowly. She moaned and gasped in low voices as I thrust into her continuously.

"How do you feel?" I asked.

"Fuck me, oh yes."

She hasn't heard what I asked. She was enjoying the sex.

I knew I was coming and took out before the lava burst out.

She understood that and took my cock in and I fucked her mouth.

Then it happened. My white lava came exploding into her mouth. She swallowed the whole cum without even wasting a single drop.

We were tired now. I wanted a seconds round but before that I thought a small rest would be better.

"You were so wild." I said. "Your husband?" I stopped in between.

"He left after a week of marriage. He didn't have much leave to stay back. I wasn't satisfied enough."

"Don't worry now I am here. I will satisfy you sexual needs." I said as I kissed her lips.

Intentions

My name is Akhila. I am a housewife. My husband is a businessman. He is successful and busy. He was on tour regularly.

He loved me very much but he wasn't much interested in physical intimacy.

He did it occasionally like a machine which never made me satisfied. I was just a hole for him to release his cream.

He gives me a peck which can't be called even a kiss. He hardly touches my breasts. He never kisses my cunt. He never even allows me to suck his cock.

He finished his work in less than three minutes and go to sleep.

I was so disappointed. I watched some videos and had to self satisfied myself.

It was one of those days; I was watching a porn video.

My fingers were inside my cunt going in and out with great speed.

I was all alone in the house. My legs were wide open, skirt over my body and a table fan directed towards my cunt.

I can feel the heat of my breaths and the sweet aroma of my wet cunt. I licked my fingers covered in my slimy honey.

I mouthed a banana and made its outer wet and inserted into my cunt. I pushed it deep and pulled back.

At that moment the calling bell went on. I cursed whoever came at the door and stood up.

It was a salesman with some cosmetics and books.

We seated at the porch. I thought I will spend some time looking at them.

He had a big bag. He was around 25. He looked tantalizing.

I picked up a perfume from his bag. I was about to ask the price when I noticed he was looking at my belly.

I was wearing a sari and my belly was clearly open. I quickly corrected my sari.

He looked down troubled. I felt like tempting him more. I wanted to see his nervousness when he sees more.

I bent even more to take out a book when the sari slipped off my shoulders.

He could see my breasts through the low neck blouse. Maybe even my cream colored bra too.

Unhurriedly I rose up and pulled back my sari. I saw his stare through the side of my eyes. A smile twinkled between my lips.

I saw a slight vibration between his legs and I was sure he has got his rod hardened.

The thought made me horny.

I saw sweat beads on his forehead.

"You want some water, right."

"Ye…yes madam." He stuttered.

"Come inside with your things. Let us sit under the air."

I brushed his hand while giving the glass of water and gave him a luscious smile. Before taking the glass back I leaned towards him and gave a kiss on his cheeks.

He wasn't expecting that. He looked at me surprised.

I locked the front door and slowly removed my sari. He stared at my exposed abdomen and the belly button.

I invited him with my hands.

Like an obedient slave he came towards me and kneeled in front of me. He dug his head into my belly and kissed my belly button.

He tongued inside the navel and licked all over my tummy.

Then he stood up and cupped my face in his hands and kissed on my lips.

He nibbled my lips and tongue as we enjoyed the steaming union of our lips.

Honestly he was doing everything that my husband never did.

His one hand was behind my head and the other was on my ass pressing them with excitement.

He unhooked my blouse and removed it from my body. He greedily looked at my bra covered tits.

His face was in between the tits in the next instant. I unbuckled my bra for him and he took it off too.

He looked at my bare breasts for a moment and started sucking the nipples like a baby.

He licked, sucked and nibbled with a sensual passion as when he took his head up I saw my tits were reddened.

He undressed in front of me. He was more than he looked. His muscled body was exquisite. He had a long cock which stood erect teasing me.

I couldn't take my eyes off the hard pole twitching itself with lust.

I couldn't wait. I kneeled in front of him and kissed its cute head. I licked the long pole from head to root and mouthed it.

He pushed the cock inside and it touched my throat. I sucked his cock as he pushed it inside with force hitting deep inside my throat.

We went to the bed. I lay on my back. He kissed me again after climbing on top of me.

He nibbled my tits with great enthusiasm.

He bit my nipples softly. My nipples were hard like his cock.

His hand untied my skirt and pulled it down.

He turned me over and started to kiss my ass. He opened my ass cheeks and licked my butt hole. He was biting the cheeks in between. I moaned with pleasure.

I was again on my back and he started licking my moist cunt.

Ahh, I never felt so good before. He was like an expert with his mouth and tongue. I felt my honey skimming down and he licked most of it.

He opened my legs wide and lay on top of me. He rammed his long pole inside my cunt.

I hugged him tight and closed my eyes.

He pushed his cock again and again with force. The way he moved gave me a conclusion that he was good. He must be probably married, I thought.

I was panting as I was almost nearing my climax. I clutched a pillow and scratched his back as I had the best orgasm in my life.

He continued fucking me till he was about to come. He took his cock out and ran into the bathroom to release his cream in the commode.

I lay naked on the bed till he came back and dressed up.

I went to the hall room and bought a lot of items. I didn't forget to get his number. He promised he will be visiting me regularly.

He kissed my pussy again before he left. I went to my bedroom and looked in to the mirror.

I was reddened. He did an amazing work on my body. I opened my cunt lips and saw the moisture of my honey.

I can't say how much satisfied I was.

I stood in front of the mirror for a long time before going to the bathroom for a long shower.

*****_____*****

******_______******

My wife's sister

I am a married guy. I live in Delhi with my wife and two kids. Nowadays I found out that my wife is not interested in me. She seldom does sex with me.

She is not as passionate as before. She doesn't take my cock in her mouth or swallow my cum. She was earlier so wild in sex but she has cooled down a lot.

Something has changed in her.

I talked to my best friend about this and he promised me to find out the reason. He advised me to take a month's leave and stay at some other place.

I decided to go to my ancestral place. It's been years. My wife and children stayed back at Delhi as they could not miss their work and classes.

I stayed at my house for three days and then went to my wife's house.

There I saw her sister, Neelam.

She has grown to be a sexy lady. I confess my sexual desires rise up seeing her.

As their wish I decided to stay in their house for a week. I tried to get as close to Neelam.

Neelam was becoming my ultimate craving. I badly wanted to fuck her.

I saw a spark in her eyes when she looked at me. It was not a look a wife's sister. Does she also have the same craving as me? I think so.

One day when I came back after visiting a friend, Neelam was alone in the home. The others will only return in the evening, she said.

I was happy to spend some time with her. We talked a lot about her studies and her aspirations. I asked whether she has any boyfriend. She smiled but didn't give me an answer.

She was wearing a red churidar top with long slit till waist and white leggings. I could see the lining of her panties through the slit. Her panties were dark colored and was clearly visible through her leggings.

My veins were on fire.

I saw her cleavage through her low neck top. I am sure she noticed that.

"You didn't say anything about your boyfriend?" I pushed her to know more.

"I don't have." She said. But her face said otherwise.

"Have you kissed?" I moved closer to her.

"Did you have sex with him?"

I saw a hint of lust along with dread in her eyes.

In the next instant I grabbed her and engulfed in a tight hug.

She was in a state of shock.

She tried to free herself.

Her tits were squeezed against me and my hold became stronger. My hard pole was against her lower abdomen. I squashed her ass with one of my hands.

"You are my sister's husband. This is wrong." She said.

I wasn't in a mood to hear that. I was blinded by lust.

I kissed her neck as my hand was in between her as cheeks.

"Your sister is not interested in me. I think she has an affair." I whispered to her.

I turned her and groped her tits, my cock pressing against her ass.

She was so soft and untouched. I made her touch my cock and rub on it as it was hardened like iron.

She was melting, her reluctance was slowly disappearing.

I use both my hands to grip her breasts. She started to moan. I knew she was ready.

She was starting to enjoy.

I released her hold and made her turn around towards me.

I kissed her and nibbled her lips. Her hands wrapped around me. She has surrendered to her sexual urges.

I let her tongue enter in my mouth and I sucked it. She was a passionate kisser.

Both my hands were on her ass, pressing them at will.

I wanted her so badly and she also wanted me. She unzipped me and took my cock out and stroked it gently.

I took her in my arms and walked towards the bedroom. I dropped her on to the bed and removed all my clothes. She looked at my naked body.

Her eyes were wide open with excitement. Her stare was on my erect penis as it throbbed in front of her.

I removed her churidar top. She was wearing a black bra. I quickly removed her bra too to make her lovely tits free.

Ahh, what a sight!

Her pink nipples were tight. Her tits were firm.

I pressed them and felt the softness of her flesh. I felt her hard beads in my mouth as I sucked and nibbled her nipples.

I pulled off her leggings and saw a navy blue panties. She was now wearing only that panties.

I can feel the adrenaline rush looking at her. She lay on the bed like a marble statue.

I kissed on her cunt over her panties. I can sense the heat of her cunt.

Her pussy was a little swollen.

I told her to have my cock in her mouth. She was reluctant at first as this was her first time. But when I wiggled my cock in front of her eyes she took it in her mouth.

She kissed the tip first and then kept the head inside. Her lips pressed the head of my cock. I forced my cock into her mouth. She sucked my cock.

She was good for a first timer. She did well. More importantly she enjoyed my cock in her mouth.

She nibbled my balls and stroked my rod as I was feeling the best pleasure in sex.

After sometime she freed my cock from her mouth. I sucked her tits again. She pressed my head in between her breasts.

I got hold of her panties and removed it. Wow, she had such a beautiful cunt, neatly shaved and clean.

It was a little swollen.

I dug my head between her thighs. I smelled her sweet pussy and inhaled the aroma of her moist cunt. I tongued over her clit and took it in my mouth and nibbled.

She squirmed when I did that.

My tongue trailed over her slit. I opened her cunt lips and started licking. Then I chewed her cunt lips.

I couldn't wait to get inside her virgin cunt. I fingered for a few seconds before forcing my cock into it.

She twisted in the bed with pain and pleasure. I pressed my cock fully inside and started fucking her.

Her moans turned into groans and her screams increased as my speed of thrusts increased.

I fucked her again and again until I came all guns blazing inside her cunt.

She also came at the same time as her wet honey ran down from her cunt onto the bed.

I rested on her after the climax.

She wrapped her hands around me as her lips were busy kissing all over my face.

It was around 2 pm.

We went to have lunch. After lunch we had sex again.

In the night I sneaked into her room and we fucked again. Instead of a week I stayed for a month and every night we had sex.

*****_____*****

******_______******

Carnal desires

She is my best friend in office.

We used to travel together to the clients and convince them. These travels got us close.

I knew the pattern lock of her cell phone as she knew mine. She used to check my Whatsapp messages and download and watch porn secretly from some Whatsapp groups.

She was active in social media.

One day I found out that she was in love with some guy while scrolling through her text messages.

She never told me about him.

When I asked about this she gave me the details. She said she was deeply in love with and will only marry him. She was a Hindu and he was a Muslim. I knew her parents will never accept this relation.

Well, the future is what we never know.

Their relation started through facebook and blossomed through text messages. They have seen each other through facebook photos but haven't met in real life. They were planning for a meeting soon.

She admitted she liked me a lot and if she hasn't met him she would have loved me.

Those words hurt me. I asked god why I didn't meet her before him.

One day she came to me with an unusual request.

Mridula and the boy, Salam had planned to meet at some place and she wanted me to go with her. The place was far away, more than three hours travel by bus and she was unsure of going there alone.

She has never travelled such long distances alone. And she felt some insecurity in meeting him alone.

On a Sunday we went to the bus station. We bought mango juice and some chips along with some dates before entering the bus.

We sat together. She tugged her hands around my hand and made it rest over her firm breast.

I felt heat between my legs.

Did she do on purpose, I didn't know.

She wasn't thinking of that. She leaned over me and was talking about a lot of things. We shared the chips and mango juice. She was enjoying my jokes and smiled wholeheartedly.

We looked a couple. A happy couple.

She was playful.

Three hours went like three minutes. I felt the journey ended even before it started.

Before alighting from the bus she asked to be at a safe distance away. She didn't want her boyfriend to see me.

He may think that she has two boyfriends.

I agreed, sadly.

She walked ahead of me. I carried the carriage bag with chips and juice. I hurried my way to the farthest corner of the bus station where I could get a clear view of her.

I saw the guy. He was handsome. His features were good and definitely he scored over me.

I saw her smiling with his chatter.

I thought he was cracking better jokes than me.

Yes, I was feeling jealous. I felt the urge to smoke. Though it was prohibited to smoke in public places, I bought a cigarette and blew out my frustration hiding behind a bus.

I could see her well. I saw her eyes searching for me.

I stood there for more than 90 minutes. I smoked five cigarettes in that time.

I am not a regular smoker you know. I am an occasional smoker. I only smoke after I have two or three pegs.

After those fucking 90 minutes I got a text saying that she is going with Salam to his house to meet his parents. She asked me to go home as Salam will give her a ride back home.

Fuck Salam, I thought.

Was I sad or angry or lost? I had no idea. I smoke two more cigarettes in succession as I saw her going with him.

At that moment a hand patted on my shoulder from behind.

Fuck, police!

My cigarette was burned more than half and I had to throw it away. I had to pay the fine for smoking at a public place. I know that fine will go to his pocket but a fine is a fine and I must pay it.

After paying the fine I walked towards the next bus to my home. I boarded the bus and I got another text. I thought to ignore it at first but how can I do that.

It said that Salam's friend was involved in an accident and he has dropped her at the bus station. She wanted to know whether I left already.

My heart jumped with joy.

I ran out of the bus and placed a call into her cell. I asked her where she was standing and walked towards her.

But the thought of Salam was haunting my mind and I was unable to show a happy face to her.

She understood that in an instant.

She asked to take her to the nearby beach. She was trying to cheer me up.

On the way we entered two or three temples and prayed together.

Well, I didn't, but I was silent. I don't know what she asked for herself from the gods.

As we walked she was leaning onto me. Her breasts were brushing my arms repeatedly.

I wondered why she didn't notice that.

She was someone else's girl but when she was with it felt like she was my girl. She behaved like I am almost her boyfriend. Almost!

We were at the beach now. We walked to the far end of the beach which was occupied mostly by couples.

Her words and behavior and her closeness to me was touching my heart. It was like she forgot about Salam.

I was changing. My mood was changing.

She jumped on my back wrapping her hands around my neck and asked me to carry her to the sea.

Her tits were squeezed against my back. I was feeling aroused.

I took her to sea. She loosened her hold as her breasts brushed my entire back while she landed on her feet.

She ran a few steps into the sea.

I stared at her like I was seeing her for the first time.

She turned towards me and splashed some salt water across my face. I ran towards her and she ran ahead. I grabbed her waist and picked her up.

I was feeling nervous to be honest.

I wasn't prepared for this day, especially after her meeting with Salam.

I didn't want to release the hold but I had to.

She was enjoying the time with me.

We saw the other couples kissing and hugging and doing other things.

She looked at me and asked do I need also something like that.

I looked at her eyes and saw her carnal desires provoking me.

I asked, are you comfortable with that.

She replied I don't mind having some fun with you. What's wrong in hugging and kissing you?

She walked towards a rock and pulled me towards her.

She slowly reached my lips and gave a gentle kiss.

I wrapped my hands around her. She was suddenly all fired up.

Her kiss became passionate and wild as she nibbled my lips, bit gently and sucked my tongue.

She was desperate.

I felt her body thirsty for more.

We forgot about Salam. Our lips united with ardor. Our tongues intertwined in our mouths. Our saliva mixed and our bodies quivered.

Her hugs became tight and she squashed her breasts against my chest. Our hips were joined together. We stood there like that for some time.

Then she released me with beaming eyes.

She saw a smile in my lips. Then she saw the bulge in front of my trousers.

She mocked me. "What is this? I was stabbing me."

I faked my anger and said. "That is a spear."

"I want to see the spear, Shiva."

"No."

"Please. I really want to see the spear."

In a moment I thought about Salam.

She asked again. "I really wish to see."

Fuck Salam. "See for yourself." I said.

She pushed me towards the rock and looked around to see anyone watching us.

She bent down and reached for the zip. She unzipped my trousers and took my hard rod out of my drawers.

She winked at me with a smile and caressed my rod and stroked it gently. It became rock hard inside her fist.

She kissed the tip and trailed around its head. My hands were between her long hairs watching her doing amazing things to my rod.

She took it into her mouth and stroked. I felt her tongue brushing my cock as she stroked continuously with her mouth.

Was I feeling love or lust or was it just my carnal desires taking over, I didn't know.

I loved what she was doing with my cock.

I knew if she continues doing like this I will erupt into her mouth. An unknown guilt was rising in my heart.

"Let's stop now." I said forcing her to free my cock.

"This is my spear now. You can close your eyes and pretend nothing is happening." She took the pole again in her mouth.

She took it deep as it touched her throat.

I was feeling all the pleasures of the world.

She took it out of her mouth and stroked my salivated rod with her fist. She licked my testicles, kissed them and nibbled them.

She was not her at that time. Her carnal urges were driving her crazy.

Sometimes my rod was in her hands and then in her mouth.

I couldn't do anything. I wanted more. I didn't want her to stop.

I held her head and pushed along with her tempo.

I moaned and groaned as I was nearing climax.

I knew my cream coming.

At the same time she increased her speed. My cock was in her mouth. I couldn't take it out in time. I came in her mouth.

She didn't spit. Instead she kept it in her mouth as I drained all my cream.

She licked my cock as he was going back to its usual form, soft and cold.

I saw her perspiring in the heat. It was 3 in the afternoon. She worked hard to get me into climax.

At that moment I concluded she was the one downloading porn from my Whatsapp groups.

"You have a lot of cream in you, Shiva. I want it again and again." She said, snickering at me.

I wondered what to say.

"Let's go now." she said.

We had to travel three hours to reach home.

She slept on my shoulders holding my hands to her breast.

She called me at night and we talked a lot about the day and my cock. She said she want to suck it again and again.

She said she liked me a lot and that was the reason she did what she did and she will always do it for me. When I asked about Salam she disconnected the call. I called her again but she switched it off.

After that day we used to hug and kiss before and after the office hours. It became a routine. She grabbed my cock whenever she got a chance.

We had no secrets between us. I saw her still messaging Salam. She was still in love with him. Am I just a passing fantasy?

She was an enigma to me. Or is she loving him but teasing me as I am her toy for lust?

I checked her messages again to see how her relation was going on with Salam. It was going strong. The guy seemed nice and decent.

One month later she invited me to her home for her sister's engagement.

The invitation was only for me. I knew she hasn't informed Salam also.

I went to her home. She asked me to come home directly. I was a bit late and my cell phone was ringing continuously with her calls.

When I reached her home she was alone. Everyone has already left.

She cribbed and complained of my irresponsibility but when I hugged her tight she became happy.

"Shiva, you were late purposely for only this."

She was wearing a red knee length top with long slit reaching even above her waist and pink leggings.

"How am I looking? Am I sexy?" she asked playfully.

She knew where my stare was at. I was looking the lining of her panties which was clearly visible above the skin tight leggings.

She lifted the back piece of the top high enough for me to see her ass. I saw the beauty of her through her tight dress.

"You like it, my ass. What do you think?"

To be honest, I lost my control. Fire burned in my veins and my cock throbbed inside my trousers. I couldn't take my eyes off the two amazing semi spheres of her back. Her butt was well shaped.

"Can I touch?" I asked; my throat was dry.

"You don't need my permission, do you?"

I grabbed them in an instant. I bent and kissed her ass over her garment.

"Don't you want to kiss m front too?" she asked lusciously.

Oh, she wanted that.

I can feel the heat of her pussy as I kissed her cunt repeatedly.

"We are getting late for the engagement." She reminded me.

We left her home instantly. She sat behind me on my motor bike hugging me tight. Her firm tits were pressed against my back. Her one arm wrapped around me and the other rested on my throbbing cock.

"I wish I could take your spear now in my mouth." Her voice was euphoric.

We arrived at the temple on time.

After the engagement she introduced me to her family. It was a low key affair. There were hardly hundred people attending the ceremony.

We had lunch together.

I had a feeling that she was introducing me as her boyfriend. Soon most of her relatives left. Her family and I were left.

I asked her permission to leave. She said she wanted a short ride with me before I leave.

We left the home and she showed her beautiful village to me.

Then it suddenly rained. We saw an old house nearby. I took my bike there. We ran to the porch of the house. It was abandoned.

Shrubs grew all around the house. There were trees with lot of branches. The sky was dark and the rain was getting heavy.

We were drenched in the rain. I saw the rain drops dripping from her head. Droplets were on her upper lips.

Suddenly she hugged me tight. Her warm breath hit my chest. I also wrapped my hands around her tightly.

Our carnal desires were rising.

My cock was throbbing as it was like an aching snake searching a hole to hide.

We were out of control now. She filled my face with her warm kisses. She breasts were rising fast as her breaths became quick.

She unbuttoned my shirt and kissed my chest and abdomen. Her tongue circled around my nipples.

My hands ran all over her back.

Her lips were on mine. She nibbled my lips and tongue. She bit my lower lips hard. I felt really bad pain and screamed.

"I want it now Shiva." she cried.

My cock was exerting pressure at her front.

I turned her around and my cock squashed between her butt cheeks. I kissed her ears and the back of her neck. My arms wrapped around her belly. I lifted her top a little and hand snaked its way through the slit on to her belly button. I circled my finger inside her belly button as she pushed her ass back to give more pressure onto my hard rod.

I unzipped her dress from behind.

She removed the top and I stared at her beautiful breasts hiding inside a white bra.

I grabbed them and started to squeeze them.

Her hands were searching between my legs. She got hold of my rod and she undid my trousers.

Her sultry gasps were heating up.

I removed her bra to free her half round wonders. They looked firm but were soft like soap bubbles. I kissed them, licked the nipples and sucked and nibbled like a fanatic. Her tits turned red after I lifted my face from them.

Mridula was stroking my cock with passion.

My trousers and briefs were half down. I quickly removed my unbuttoned shirt and half pulled trousers and under garment. I stood bare in front of her.

She pulled her leggings down and threw it away into some corner of the porch.

She looked lustier in her blue panties. She had an amazing body.

I pushed the front door of the house. We heard something clanging to the door. I pushed again with more force. The door opened. I saw the lock on the floor.

We went inside. She took a broom and seeped a corner of the room.

She threw the broom away and slept on the floor. She was ready to have sex. She wanted it badly. I wanted it badly.

Nothing else mattered, just me, her and our carnal desires.

I looked at her admiring the beauty of her well crafted figure. She wasn't too thin, but fleshy. Her curves were perfect. Her breasts were round and solid. Her hair spread across the floor. Her horny face was beaming with beauty. Her thighs looked like ivory tusks. The blue panties added a sensual splendor to her.

"I don't want to forget this day Shiva."

"You will never forget." I promised.

I was on top of her. My lips met hers.

I removed her panties and lowered my head between her thighs.

I kissed her slit and nibbled her clit.

"Aaaaahhhh." She screamed with lust.

I nibbled her clit continuously as she wriggled with pleasure. I opened the petals of her rose flower and my tongue trailed up and down her cunt.

She lifted her hips, her eyes were tightly closed and she squirmed and moaned.

"Shiva… I want your spear… it is mine… spear in my mouth…" She blabbered.

I turned 180 degrees and was on all four. My cock touched her face and she took it inside her mouth. I pushed it deep inside her mouth and I could feel the tip entering her throat. I rammed continuously into her head, slow but deep.

My head was between her thighs licking her cunt. A strong scent along with heat was coming from her cunt.

"Shiva, fuck me, I want it now." she moaned. It was hard for me to understand what she was saying as my cock was entering and exiting her mouth with easy movements.

I know I shouldn't waste my time.

She is my girl and I should claim her first.

I returned to my normal position and lay over her partially. I guided my cock into her wet cunt. She parted her legs wide. Her cunt was tight and I forced my rod. It was hard like iron. She wriggled with pain. She shrieked loud but was silenced by a thunder.

The rain was getting heavy outside the house.

I pushed again with greater force and my cock head was inside. She cupped her cunt and screamed.

I waited for a moment. "Don't stop I want the spear inside." She was panting.

I took a deep breath and pushed again. My cock was a quarter inside her cunt and I heard her scream aloud.

I squeezed her breasts and locked my lips with hers and I tried to insert my rod deeper into her tight and moist cunt.

I felt her squirming under my body. I retracted a bit as the cock had only its head now inside her cunt and rammed with full force.

Her body twitched and she but hardly on my lips making a cut. We both felt the taste of blood in our mouths.

I slowly pulled my hips back and pushed again. And again. And again.

She sucked my lips and the blood. I increased my speed and she groaned with each push. She cupped my butt cheeks.

"You wanted this spear, have it."

"Yes this is my spear." She was twisting with pain.

Now the movements were easy. I hit her insides continuously with more force and speed. She shrieked with each thrust.

I felt I was about to come and removed my cock in an instant. I came over her thighs.

She was panting heavily.

"Your spear is amazing Shiva." She was rubbing her clit. I inserted my fingers inside and pushed and pulled them rapidly. In a few minutes she squirted. Her honey spurted out as from a water jet.

"That was great fun." She said.

"The fun is about to start." I snickered. I can hear the thunder rumbling in the skies and the rain pelting down heavily. "I am going to do again. You want to remember this day forever, don't you?"

She looked at me with lust as she wiped my cream from her thighs and licked.

"Oh yes." She said. "Give me my spear."

She took it again in her mouth. My cream was still at the tip. She licked the head and trailed all over the cock body and nibbled my balls. She stroked my rod with her hands.

I kept her head still and pushed my rod into her mouth. By the time it was hard again. I kept pushing into her mouth.

When I tried to take it out she demanded she want my cream in her mouth. I pressed deep into her mouth and my cock was touching her throat.

I made her lie again and rammed again into her moist cunt. She moaned loudly. I was not going to stop. I was going in again and again and she cried out with both pain and pleasure.

She has surrendered to me as my cock was continuously exploring her honey soaking cunt.

I took my cock out as I was nearing climax. She nibbled my balls again before taking 'her spear' in her mouth.

I came in her mouth filling her mouth with my cream. She sucked even the last drop from my cock and swallowed.

I helped her rise on her feet and bent forward to lick her cunt. I opened her pussy lips and licked her cunt. I nibbled the clit and cunt lips as she was reaching towards ecstasy.

I inserted my fingers and shook them vigorously while she rubbed her clit. She came spilling her honey from her cunt. I licked her honey as she had orgasm.

We both smelled of cream and honey.

We walked out into the rain and washed ourselves. The whole area was vacant and we kissed in the rain.

We hugged in the rain and my hands were squeezing her ass cheeks.

"I want to do in the rain." I whispered in her ears.

"No," she said. "I am tired. My pussy is paining."

I could see the swell of her pussy.

"You asked for it. I can't stop now. The climate is driving me wild. And rain soaked Mridula standing in front of me naked is making me wilder."

She was indeed a wonderful sight.

I cupped her breasts and circled my fingers around her hard beads.

"Can I?" I asked her.

I know her cunt was burning but I really wanted to do again. I wanted her to remember every moment of this day. I wanted her to forget Salam.

She sighed. She didn't want. I thought she would deny. But she surprised me.

"Do it. You are the boss today." She took my cock in her hands and stroked it.

She was ready!

I lifted one of her leg and wrapped around her with the other hand. She helped my cock to enter her cunt.

I did again. I fucked her hard in that heavily pelting rain.

We both had our orgasms together. She rested her head on my chest. Our privates were really burning. The throb was exquisite. My cream was in her cunt and her honey soaked my rod.

I didn't take it out in time and she was also tired to say so. We stayed in the rain in the same position for a long time and then I asked.

"Don't you want this spear every day?"

She looked into my eyes. I saw a spark so unexplainable tingling in her eyes.

She hugged me tight as she was unable to face me. I wrapped my arms around her.

I heard her saying. "I love you Shiva. I want you."

That's what I wanted to hear. I know how to throw the thorn out. Salam will be fucked.

Mridula is my girl. I decided.

$$$

Can you believe that tomorrow is our wedding day?

Yes she is my bride.

*****_____*****

******_______******

All these stories are available individually as eBooks in Amazon.

DESPERATIONS

INVITATION

INTENTIONS

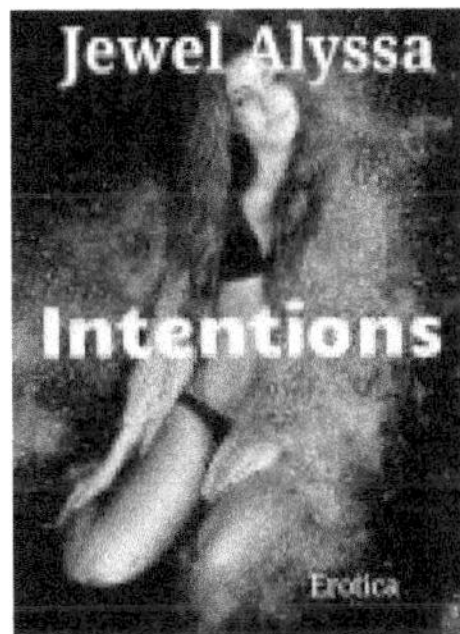

MY WIFE'S SISTER

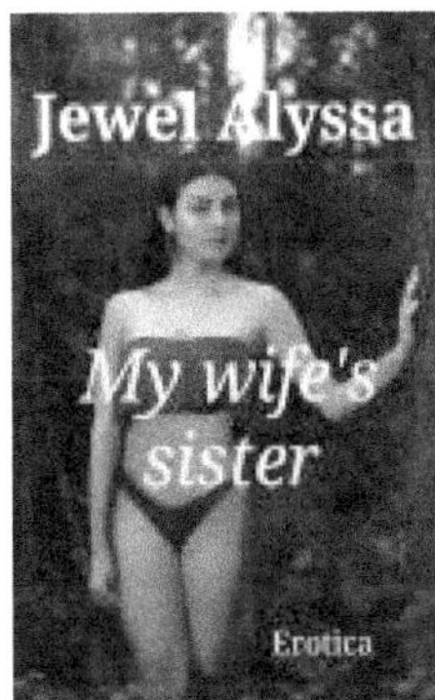

CARNAL DESIRES